STUNT BOY SAM

By Michael Wagner
Illustrated by Shane Nagle

Pearson Australia
(a division of Pearson Australia Group Pty Ltd)
707 Collins Street, Melbourne, Victoria 3008
PO Box 23360, Melbourne, Victoria 8012
www.pearson.com.au

First published 2010 by Pearson Australia
2019 2018 2017 2016
10 9 8 7 6 5 4 3 2

Publisher: Simone Calderwood
Illustrator: Shane Nagle
Editor: Steve Dobney
Designer: Glen McClay
Copyright & Pictures Editor: Caitlin O'Brien
Project Editor: Aisling Coughlan
Production Controller: Claire Henry
Printed in Australia by the SOS Print + Media Group

ISBN 978 1 4425 2928 1

Pearson Australia Group Pty Ltd ABN 40 004 245 943

Contents

CHAPTER 1

HOW TO BECOME POPULAR

THE ONLY REASON SAM DINGLE went to the skate park that Friday afternoon was because he was fairly sure no-one else would be there. After all, he was on a mission to become more popular, not to make a complete fool of himself. So, if there was even one other kid dipping in and out of those big concrete bowls, Sam would have turned around and headed straight back home.

Sam needed the skate park to himself so he could secretly learn one really good skate trick. Just one. If he could land a really difficult trick, his popularity at school would go through the roof. He knew that, because it's exactly what had happened to Taylor Walker.

After Taylor Walker rode his skateboard down the handrail at school, for two whole flights of stairs, then landed perfectly on his deck and skidded through the school gates, everyone loved him. No-one had been able to make that trick work except Taylor. And after that, he was a hero.

Standing on the edge of the giant concrete bowl, clutching his skateboard, Sam hoped to become a hero, too. But he knew his trick had to be good. It had to be more dangerous and difficult than Taylor's handrail slide. It had to be almost impossible. That was the only way Sam could ever be popular.

Even though Sam was in Year Five, he estimated himself to be the ninety-eighth most popular kid in school. And there were only a hundred kids at his school. Even some of the five-year-olds who'd just started were more popular than Sam. Actually, when Sam thought about it, all the five-year-olds were more popular than him. The only two kids less popular than Sam were his best friends, Johnson Peters and Kevin Ng.

They were even more nervous and clumsy than him, and they never knew the right thing to say to anyone.

So Sam needed to perfect the trick he'd been working on in his head for days. And the only time to do that, without the risk of making a fool of himself, was when the skate park was totally empty.

Normally the skate park would be full of kids, but it was empty that Friday because everyone from his school was at camp. Sam should have been there, too, but he'd woken up with an aching tummy on Monday morning and wasn't well enough to go. Instead, he spent the whole week at home. The one good thing about staying home was that it gave him lots of time to think up the perfect skate trick.

Sam placed his skateboard on the concrete. He pushed his helmet away from his eyes and looked down into the giant bowl. Up close, it was much deeper than he'd realised. It was deep enough to make him feel dizzy. So dizzy that he had to step back from the edge to keep his balance.

"You knew it wouldn't be easy," Sam whispered to himself. "Now get on with it."

He stepped back to the edge of the bowl and stood beside his skateboard. To start his trick, he needed to kick his deck into the air. Then, as it tumbled, he'd jump on top of it and air-surf it straight into the bowl. It was a trick so difficult that even the world's best skateboarders wouldn't try it. But he had to do something special if he was going to become an instant hero.

"You can do it," Sam whispered to himself. "Sam the man can."

That's what Sam always said to himself when he was frightened—"Sam the man can." It gave him a little more courage, a little more strength. He needed both right now.

Finally, Sam was ready to try his trick. Before he started, he quickly glanced around to check that there were no kids up on the main street watching him. A few adults were wandering along, browsing in the shop windows, and there were two babies being pushed along in prams, but there were no school kids. It was safe.

Sam turned back to the concrete bowl and took a deep breath. As he imagined himself pulling off the most daring and amazing skate trick in history, he didn't notice the long, black limousine pull up in the main street behind him. And, as Sam reminded himself of the hero he would soon become, he didn't see the limo's tinted rear window slide down.

“Three,” Sam said, counting himself in, “Two … One!”

With the toe of his runner, Sam flicked his skateboard high into the air.

CHAPTER 2

SAM'S SLICK TRICK

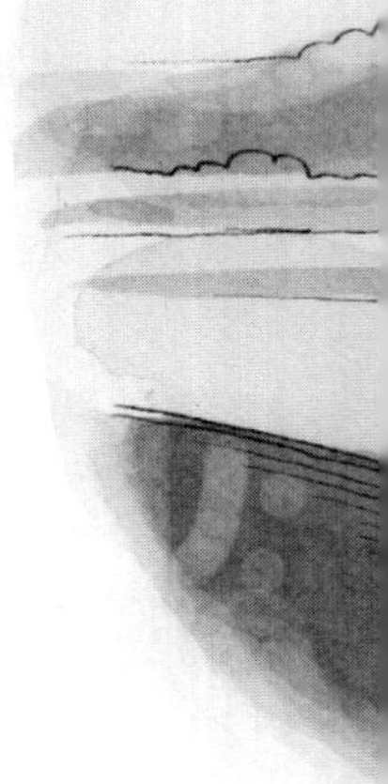

SAM LEAPT TOWARDS his skateboard as it tumbled over the edge of the huge concrete bowl. His feet landed flat on the deck's scratchy, black surface. Suddenly, he was dropping towards the smooth concrete wall.

"Ahhhhhhh!" he screamed in terror.

Sam's wheels clicked against the bowl wall, about halfway down. He held up both arms and rode his skateboard down the wall. In no time at all, he was whizzing along the floor of the bowl, then suddenly heading upwards again. To his amazement, Sam was still standing on the skateboard.

At the top of the bowl, Sam's feet and his skateboard separated. They rocketed out of the bowl in different directions. In mid-air, Sam did an accidental somersault. Beneath him, his skateboard crashed onto the concrete.

Oh no! thought Sam, as he tumbled back to earth. *This is really going to hurt!*

Thump! Sam landed flat on his bottom on top of his skateboard. After the initial bump, he found himself slowly and peacefully rolling along the flat concrete.

Sam sat there, waiting for the pain to begin. There was no way he could have completed a trick like that without hurting something. But there was no pain. Sam's trick had worked. It was perfect!

Sam jumped off his board and punched the air.

"Wait till they see that!" he yelled. "Then I'll be a star!"

At just that moment, another excited voice also yelled out.

"That was amazing, kid!"

Sam spun around to see the face of a man with long curly hair and round, red glasses, staring at him from the back seat of a black limo.

"I've never seen anything like it!" the man said. "And I've seen a lot of things!"

"Thanks," Sam said, turning away again. He didn't like talking to strangers, even if they were in the back seat of a big black limo.

"You want to be a star, kid?" the man yelled.

Sam frowned. He wondered how the man knew he wanted to be a star. Sam looked back over his shoulder, but kept well away.

The man waved a small white card through the limo window.

"I'm a movie director, kid," the man said. "My name's George Fielding. Maybe you've seen some of my films—*The Rat That Went Splat* and *The Rat That Went Splat 2*?"

Sam loved *The Rat That Went Splat*, and he didn't mind *The Rat That Went Splat 2*, either. But there was still no way he was getting any closer to that black limo. In fact, he was looking to see if there were any people wandering along the main street, just in case he needed to call out for help. Luckily, there were quite a few now.

"Anyway, I've been scouting for locations for my new movie," the man in the limo continued. "I couldn't help noticing that trick you just did. It was brilliant."

Sam smiled proudly. His new trick had already impressed one person. Imagine what the kids at school would think when they saw it.

"I need a stunt double for my new movie," the man said. "If you can do a trick like that, you'd be perfect. Here, take my card."

Sam didn't move any closer, so the man flicked his card through the window. It fluttered in the air and landed on the concrete.

"So if you're interested in being in a Hollywood movie," the man said, "this is your big chance. Think it over, kid. If your parents say it's okay, give me a call. But don't wait too long. We start filming next week. If I don't hear from you by five o'clock tomorrow afternoon, I'll have to find someone else to turn into a mega-star. Let me know, kid."

As Sam stood there, clutching his skateboard, the rear window of the limo closed smoothly. The limo pulled quietly into the traffic and drove away. Once it was all the way past the roundabout, Sam picked up the business card and had a look.

On the back of the card were four phone numbers, a fax number, a pager number, two email addresses, and three website addresses.

"Hmm," Sam said quietly to himself as he studied the card. "I wonder if he's making *The Rat That Went Splat 3*."

George Fielding
DIRECTOR
HOLLYWOOD
FEATURE
FILMS

Sam put the business card into his pocket and silently asked himself if he'd just been dreaming. Could that really have been George Fielding? Could he really end up in a Hollywood blockbuster?

Sam needed to talk all of this over with his parents, so he headed straight home with his skateboard in his arms. He knew he wasn't good enough to ride it all that way.

CHAPTER 3

IT'S UP TO MUM AND DAD

SAM HAD TO WAIT until almost dinnertime to find out if his parents would let him be a stunt double in George Fielding's movie. He'd asked his mum during the afternoon, but she had insisted on discussing it with his dad before they made a final decision.

When his dad came home, he and Sam's mum went into their bedroom to talk in private. Sam tried to listen from the hallway, but his parents went all the way into their bathroom and closed the door. So Sam just sat on his bed and waited.

Finally, his mum and dad came in and sat on the end of his bed.

"Sam," his mum said, "before we agree to you being a stunt double in a Hollywood movie, we really need to ask Mr Fielding a few important questions. Is that okay, sweetheart?"

"Can you ring him right now?" Sam asked, handing his mum the director's business card.

"Why not," Sam's mum said with a smile.

As Sam and his dad sat at the kitchen bench, Mrs Dingle dialled Mr Fielding's mobile number.

Mr Dingle punched Sam on the shoulder lightly and said, "So you're going to be a big star, Sammy? Who would have predicted that?"

"Not me," Sam said, giving his dad a playful punch on the leg.

"Is that George Fielding?" Mrs Dingle asked into the phone. "Oh, hello Mr Fielding. It's lovely to talk to you. My name's Felicity Dingle. I'm the mother of Sam Dingle. He says you spoke to him at the skate park this afternoon."

As Sam and his dad listened excitedly, Mrs Dingle chatted with Mr Fielding for several minutes.

She asked him all sorts of questions about the movie he was making and the role he had in mind for Sam. Then she thanked him very much and hung up.

"Well?" Sam and his dad said.

"It seems okay," Mrs Dingle said, nodding. Then a broad smile appeared on her face and she added, "I think our boy's about to become a movie star."

Sam leapt out of his chair and gave his mum a big hug. His dad joined in too.

When the Dingles had calmed down, the three of them sat at the kitchen table for a dinner of meatloaf, mashed potatoes and peas. It was Sam's favourite meal and they always had it when they were celebrating.

"Did Mr Fielding say who I'm stunt-doubling for?" Sam asked his mum. He was keen to know which amazing actor he would be playing in the movie. He was hoping it would be Jack Kroozer or Max Tannick. They were his

favourite movie stars. But he'd be happy if it was Zack Teflon or Brandon Powers, because they were pretty cool, too.

"He wouldn't say, sweetheart," Sam's mum replied. "He said everything about the movie is top secret until it comes out in six months' time. The only clues he gave me were that the actor is a really big star and that your body shapes are similar."

As Sam chewed a mouthful of meatloaf, he wondered which movie stars would have a body like an eleven year old boy—especially one who's short and skinny. His dad must have been wondering the same thing, because he suddenly said, "A lot of movie stars are small. They look big on the screen, but in real life they're quite tiny."

"I've heard that," Mrs Dingle agreed.

Sam wondered if Jack Kroozer was little, like him.

"So what did you do that impressed Mr Fielding, Sam?" Mr Dingle asked.

"Oh, just a skateboard trick," Sam said through a mouthful of peas.

Mr Dingle shook his head in wonder and said, "I didn't realise you were so good at skateboarding."

"Neither did I," Sam replied, scooping peas onto his fork.

"All I know is we're very proud of you, Sam," Mrs Dingle said, patting her son's shoulder. "Aren't we, Jack?"

"We sure are," Mr Dingle agreed, spitting a crumb of meatloaf onto the table. "Whoops."

Sam sat back in his chair and grinned. He'd only done one skateboard trick and already his life had improved incredibly.

CHAPTER 4

CAN I HAVE YOUR AUTOGRAPH?

THINGS WERE REALLY looking up for Sam Dingle. He was going to be in a movie. His parents were proud of him. But that was nothing compared to what happened when he arrived at school the following Monday morning.

Over the weekend, Sam had sent texts to his friends, Johnson and Kevin, about what had happened at the skate park. They'd then told their parents, and their parents had told other parents... By the time Monday morning came around, everyone knew. Which is why, when

Sam walked through the school gates at 8.30 a.m., he was mobbed!

"Look!" yelled Vincent from Year Two. "It's him!"

Every kid in the school ran towards Sam. It was like a stampede. Sam backed away until he was right up against the school fence. In an instant, he was surrounded. Ninety-nine kids yelled at him at the same time. Six teachers did, too. Everyone had a question about the movie. They all wanted to touch Sam. They wanted his photograph. And his autograph. They shoved things in front of him and asked him to sign them.

"Can you sign my notepad?" Vanessa Giazi yelled.

"And my maths book!" Tony Phong shouted.

"And my arm!" Chloe Ward begged.

"And my face!" cried Rachel Witherspoon.

School started an hour later than usual that day because Sam wanted to sign things for everyone. He loved being this popular and he didn't want to disappoint anyone.

"Who are you going to be in the movie?" asked little Acorn, from Year One.

"It's a secret until the movie comes out," replied Sam.

"Wow," Acorn said, her eyes as wide as dinner plates. "A secret. A real secret. Not just a made-up one."

"All I know," Sam continued, "is that the actor is a big Hollywood star. And we have the same body shape."

"Maybe it's Zack Teflon," Acorn suggested.

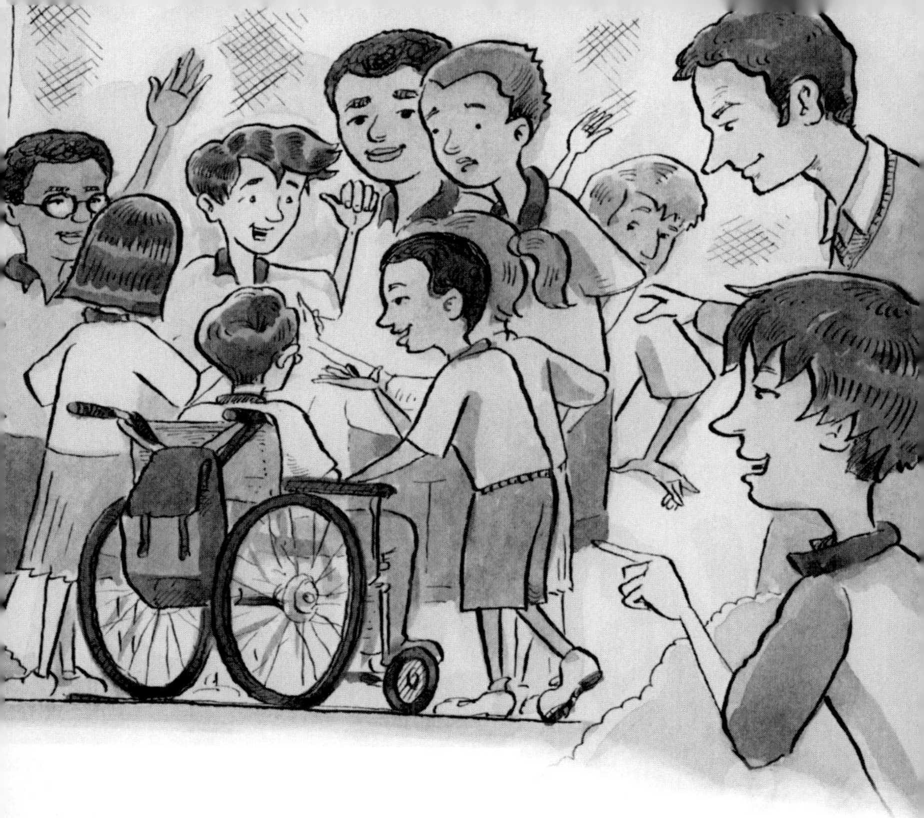

Then she ran away, yelling, "It's Zack Teflon! It's Zack Teflon!"

"It could be Jack Kroozer," Georgia Jones suggested. "He's skinny and people say he's little."

"Maybe it's a child actor," Mrs Fury called out from the back of the crowd. "You know, a teenager like Sebastian Crayon."

Several girls gasped. Sam raised his eyebrows. He hadn't thought of Sebastian Crayon.

"I hope it's him," Sam said, nodding. "He's cool."

"Just like you," Beatrice Clover said, fluttering her eyelashes at Sam.

Wow! thought Sam. *Everyone loves me.*

CHAPTER 5

TOUGH TREVOR TO THE RESCUE

FOR THE WHOLE DAY, everyone was nice to Sam. Thirty-seven kids offered him the tastiest treats from their lunch boxes. He was given drinks, chocolate biscuits, chips, lolly bags and even a whole birthday cake. Alice Riccardi's mum had made the cake for Alice's class to share, but they all voted to give it to Sam instead.

The prettiest girl in school, Tania Worsley, asked Sam if he'd be her date at the school dance.

"But we don't have a school dance," Sam said.

"I know, silly," laughed Tania. "I want you to promise to be my date if we ever *do* have a school dance."

Sam nodded his head enthusiastically. In his wildest dreams, he never thought he'd be asked on a date by Tania Worsley. Even if it was a date that would probably never happen.

The teachers were nice to Sam, too, especially Miss Prince, the drama teacher. "Perhaps you could mention me to Mr Fielding when you see him, Sam," she said, flicking back her hair.

Even Tough Trevor Merchant, the school bully, was kind to Sam. Instead of making dumb jokes about Sam, as he usually did, Trevor offered to be his personal bodyguard. He kept the autograph-hunters away from Sam, Johnson and Kevin, so they could share out all of Sam's extra lunch treats in private. Sam gave Tough Trevor half a cake as a tip. He ate it in three mouthfuls.

"Maybe you're going to play Max Tannick," Tough Trevor said, cake crumbs tumbling down his chin.

"He's the toughest actor in Hollywood. Did you see him in *Alien Robot 2*?"

Sam and his friends looked at each other. None of them had seen *Alien Robot 2*. Their parents wouldn't let them.

"We're not allowed to see those kinds of movies," Sam said, bravely.

Normally, at that moment, Tough Trevor would have pelted all three boys with insults for being such wimps, but that day he didn't. He just slapped them on the back and said, "I guess I shouldn't watch movies like that either. They are kind of gross."

That's how it was all day long for Sam Dingle. At school, he could do no wrong. It was the same the next day, and for the rest of the week. The following week, Sam didn't turn up to school at all.

That was because he was needed on the set of a major Hollywood film.

CHAPTER 6

SAM GETS A SHOCK

ON THE MORNING OF THE FILM SHOOT, Sam and his parents walked to the skate park. They were told to meet Mr Fielding and the rest of the film crew there at 9 a.m. When they arrived, they found the skate park was roped off and hundreds of people were watching as the film crew set up for the day.

Inside the ropes were lots of security guards, several big caravans, dozens of people rushing around, chairs with words like "Director" and "Producer" written on the back of them, and lots of equipment including cameras, lights and microphones.

When Sam and his parents approached one of the security guards, Mr Fielding rushed over and shook Sam's hand.

"Here's my super stunt double," Mr Fielding said, his round red glasses perched on the very tip of his nose.

"Hi," Sam said, feeling a little worried about the number of people around.

"Let's get you into make-up," Mr Fielding said, leading Sam past the security guard and through the ropes.

Mr and Mrs Dingle tried to follow their son, but the giant security guard locked the rope back into place.

"Aren't we allowed in, too?" Sam's dad asked Mr Fielding.

"I'm really sorry, Mr Dingle," Mr Fielding said, "but this is a closed shoot. Only the cast and crew are allowed to watch. Shortly, we'll be putting up screens all around the skate park, so no-one can see what we're filming. We can't risk the general public finding out about this movie, and the amazing stars involved. I hope you understand."

"We do," Mrs Dingle said, nodding sadly. "When should we come back to collect Sam?"

"Four o'clock," Mr Fielding said, patting Sam on the shoulder. "That should be enough time for us to make him a big movie star."

Sam's mum and dad leaned over the ropes to give Sam another family hug. Then they waved goodbye and left for the day.

A few minutes later, in one of the caravans, a lady with spiky black hair asked Sam to sit in a chair. She wanted to do his make-up.

"Make-up!" Sam said, feeling alarmed as the black-haired woman wrapped him in a gown.

"Relax," the lady said. "All the big stars wear make-up, including the men."

"What about Jack Kroozer?" Sam asked

"He wears more than most," the lady replied.

Sam wasn't keen on make-up, but if it was good enough for Jack Kroozer, he'd give it a go. He relaxed back in his seat and closed his eyes so the lady could pat, brush and draw make-up all over his face.

When the lady was done, Sam was dying to see how he looked, but just as he opened his eyes, she swung his chair around and pushed him towards a special changing room at the back of the caravan.

"He's all yours, Po!" she called out.

Po, a big woman in a purple dress, shook Sam's hand. Then she led him into a small booth that was surrounded by black curtains.

"Now," Po said, through the black curtains, "it's time to get your costume organised. Just strip down to your underwear, then put on the garment that's hanging over the stool. Give me a yell when you're ready."

"Okay," Sam said, nervously. He didn't realise he would have to strip down to his underwear.

He picked up the white garment and wondered what it was. He'd never seen anything like it.

"Are you ready?" Po called.

"Nearly," Sam called back.

He quickly stripped down and put on the weird garment. It looked a bit like a ladies' one-piece bathing suit. It went down to his knees and up over his shoulders.

"Are you decent?" Po called.

"I guess," Sam replied nervously.

The black curtain swung open. Po grabbed Sam's wrist and pulled him out of the booth.

"Foot up," Po ordered, getting Sam to step into his costume.

When she finished doing up the zip at the back, Sam looked down at himself.

He wasn't sure what he was wearing. It was dark green and made of velvet. It looked like a robe. But then he was also wearing a helmet, with a wig poking out from under it.

He wondered if he was meant to be a skateboarding pirate, or maybe a hovercraft racer from the future.

When Sam slipped his feet into a pair of pink runners, Po announced that he was done.

She asked if he'd like to see how he looked. Sam nodded. He was dying to get the full view.

Po took him back to the make-up mirror and then spun him around. Sam saw himself for the first time. For a moment, he couldn't work out what he was meant to be. Then he realised.

"I'm in a dress!" he said.

"Of course," Po replied, straightening the dress across his shoulders.

"I've got wrinkles all over my face!" Sam said. "I look like a granny!"

"Not just any granny," Po said, proudly.

"But I don't want to be a granny!" Sam said, suddenly noticing that he had two large, fake bumps on his chest. "I want to be a cool actor!"

"I beg your pardon, young man," Po said. "You just happen to be stunt-doubling for one of the finest Hollywood actors of all time. Vera May is still a massive star at the age of eighty-seven!"

That didn't make Sam feel any better. All he could think about were his friends at school and what they would say when they found out he was a stunt double for a granny!

"We need our stunt double!" a woman yelled as she leaned in through the caravan door.

Po steered Sam out of the caravan, saying, "Go get 'em, Skater Granny!"

CHAPTER 7

MEET YOUR STUNT DOUBLE

"YOU LOOK GREAT, SAM," Mr Fielding said. He and Sam were standing in front of the skate park, surrounded by people, lights and cameras.

"I didn't know I was playing a …" Sam muttered, before the director turned away and yelled.

"Miss May!" Mr Fielding called out. "Come and have a look at your stunt double!"

Sam looked past Mr Fielding to see an old lady, dressed just like him, wandering towards them. He recognised her immediately.

"Don't yell at me, young man!" Vera May said, scowling at Mr Fielding. "I'm not deaf!"

"Sorry, Miss May," Mr Fielding said, "I just thought you'd like to meet Sam. He's your stunt double in the skate park scene."

Mr Fielding pushed Sam forward so Vera May could have a good look at him.

Standing in front of her, Sam could see that they were exactly the same height and build. All he had to do was hunch his shoulders and they'd look like twins.

"He'll do," said Vera May, before marching back to the biggest caravan and slamming the door behind her.

Mr Fielding clapped twice and called out, "Set up for the final scene!"

Then he leaned down to Sam and said, "All you have to do is repeat the trick you did the other day. We just need one good shot of that trick and we'll have the perfect end to our film. That shouldn't be too hard, should it Sam?"

Sam nodded. Then he realised he should have been shaking his head, so he quickly did that as well.

"Great," Mr Fielding said, patting Sam's shoulder. Then he yelled, "Give the stunt double his skateboard!"

A skateboard was shoved into Sam's hands. The black-haired lady quickly drew three more lines on his face.

Po straightened his dress one last time. Then everyone stood back, leaving Sam at the edge of the concrete bowl with a skateboard in his arms.

"Action!" yelled Mr Fielding.

CHAPTER 8

SKATE FOR YOUR LIFE, SAM!

THIS WAS IT. This was Sam's big moment. He took a deep breath and put his skateboard down beside the bowl.

I'm a granny, he thought to himself. *A granny! There goes my popularity.*

Sam stood back and pushed the long, grey hair out of his eyes.

And I don't even know if I can do this trick again, he thought to himself. *That other time might've been a fluke. I might never be able to repeat it!*

"We're rolling, Sam!" yelled Mr Fielding. "Any time you're ready!"

As Sam stared into the concrete bowl, he felt like running away. All his popularity was about to disappear and he was almost certainly going to make a total fool of himself in front of all these film people.

"Let's go, Sam!" called out Mr Fielding, sounding slightly impatient.

Oh well, thought Sam. *There's no turning back now.* Then he whispered the only thing he could think of that might help.

"Sam… the man… can."

Sam closed his eyes and counted himself in.

"Three… Two… One!"

With the toe of his pink runner, Sam flicked his skateboard high into the air. He hurled himself after it, his feet hitting the deck in mid-air. He stayed on the board as he fell towards the bowl wall. His wheels slammed against the concrete, almost making him fall, but he held out both arms and glided to the bottom of the bowl. Suddenly, Sam and his skateboard were shooting up the opposite wall. They rocketed out of the bowl and into mid-air again.

His skateboard went one way, and Sam went another.

Once again he did an accidental somersault then tumbled back to earth. But this time, he was the wrong way around. There was no way he could land safely on his bottom.

"Ahhh!" Crash!

Sam hit his skateboard hard with the top of his helmet. He reached out to steady himself and grabbed his deck. He was rolling along on the concrete doing a headstand. His skateboard hit the edge of the grass and came to a sudden stop, making Sam fall flat on his tummy. As he lay on the grass, groaning, Mr Fielding yelled, "Cut!"

Then the whole place erupted with applause. Everyone clapped and yelled as Sam climbed back to his feet and picked up his board. Mr Fielding rushed over and patted his shoulder, saying, "That was the most amazing thing I've ever seen! It was even better than the one you did the other day. Now can you just do a second take?"

Sam shook his head slowly.

"Okay," Mr Fielding said. "That take will have to do."

As Sam made his way back to the make-up caravan, everyone he passed patted him on the back. He'd done an excellent job in the film, but it didn't change the fact that he was stunt-doubling for a granny.

Mr and Mrs Dingle asked Sam about a million questions on the way home that afternoon. He answered every one as honestly as he could. Except when Mrs Dingle asked, "So who did you stunt-double for?"

Sam wondered how he should answer. He didn't want to lie, but he knew if he told anyone—including his parents—that he'd played a granny, it would get around in no time. So Sam said, "It's a secret, Mum. I'm not allowed to say until the movie comes out."

And that's exactly what Sam told the kids at school. He said that he'd done a skate trick and that he'd worn a crazy costume and that he'd met one of the biggest actors in Hollywood. But that was all he told them. The rest, he said, was a secret, right up until the movie came out in six months' time.

CHAPTER 9

THANKS, SKATER GRANNY

FOR SIX LONG MONTHS, Sam was still the most popular kid in school. But it was hard for him to enjoy it, because he knew the day would come when everyone would discover that he'd played a granny.

And, of course, that day did come …

Little Acorn had counted down the whole six months on her calendar. She knew, before anyone else, that Sam's movie was due to come out.

She was also desperate to see *Skater Granny* because it was meant to be the funniest movie in years. So, when she was sitting in the cinema, watching Vera May perform an incredible skateboard trick at a skate park that looked very familiar, she worked it all out.

And, of course, she told everyone.

When Sam arrived at school the next morning, he was mobbed again. Everyone knew he'd stunt-doubled for Skater Granny. They laughed at the fact that he'd played a little old lady. Only Acorn stood up for him.

"Skater Granny's cool," she insisted, but no-one listened.

They were too busy making fun of Sam.

Sam didn't try to defend himself. He'd known this was coming and now there was nothing he could do about it.

Oh well, he thought. *At least I had a good six months.*

But then, one by one, every kid in the school went to see *Skater Granny*. And every one of them loved it.

When they saw Sam's big trick at the end, they laughed and clapped because they thought it was incredible. And because Sam looked hilarious dressed as an old lady. And because Skater Granny was the coolest, funniest and best character any of them had ever seen. They just loved her. And they loved anyone who'd had anything to do with her amazing movie.

Including Sam.